GERRY CONWAY & ROSS ANDRU INSPIRATION TODD DEZAGO SCRIPT RON LIM PENCILS
SCOTT KOBLISH INKS DAVE SHARPE LETTERS DIGITAL RAINBOW COLORS JOHN BARBER EDITOR
MACKENZIE CADENHEAD & RALPH MACCHIO CONSULTING EDITORS JOE QUESADA EDITOR-IN-CHIEF DAN BUCKLEY PUBLISHER
COVER BY RANDY GREEN, RICK KETCHAM & CHRIS SOTOMAYOR
Time: Some say that it flows like a river, and that all of us are merely swept along in its current, for we are unable to change its flow...
...but what if someone could?
What if someone could freeze time solid...and what if that someone planned to use his ability to conquer Heaven and Earth within the space of a nano-second?
And what if there were only two heroes who could stop it? Two heroes who find themselves--
BITTEN BY AN IRRADIATED SPIDER, WHICH GRANTED HIM INCREDIBLE ABILITIES, PETER PARKER LEARNED THE ALL-IMPORTANT LESSON, THAT WITH GREAT POWER THERE MUST ALSO COME GREAT RESPONSIBILITY. AND SO HE BECAME THE AMAZING
SPIDER-MAN AND
HAILING FROM THE MYSTICAL REALM OF ASGARD AND WIELDING THE WAR HAMMER MJOLNIR, THIS GOD AMONGST MEN HAS PLEDGED HIS IMMORTAL POWER IN THE SERVICE OF MANKIND--HE IS THE MIGHTY
THOR IN
OUT OF TIME!

VISIT US AT

www.abdopub.com

Spotlight, a division of ABDO Publishing Company Inc., is the school and library distributor of the Marvel Entertainment books.

Library bound edition © 2006

Library of Congress Cataloging-in-Publication Data

Thor: Out of Time!

ISBN 1-59961-004-3 (Reinforced Library Bound Edition)

All Spotlight books are reinforced library binding
and manufactured in the United States of America

Listen to me, Looter-- I don't have time for this!
I mean, you are aware that taking people hostage and stealing millions of dollars worth of scientific equipment is against the law, right?
The Institute for SeismoHarmonic Studies...
First of all, Mr. Spidey-pants-- I'm not stealing, I'm borrowing!
I need these electromagnetic refractualizers to restore my little meteor's polarity and help us to find her geologic twin!
Here we go...
Also, these gentlemen are not hostages...

You guys do know you're free to go whenever you want, right?
Mmfrm mm! Rrmumumum! Frumm!

See?! They don't want to leave! They're eager to see the results of my genius!

Spidey, how do you get yourself into these messes?
I can't just ambush the Looter with my spider powers, 'cause he actually has super powers too-- inordinate strength he got inhaling strange gases from that meteor he's holding...

He's completely delusional, and his crazy schemes usually turn out to be duds--
--but there's no telling what he's got that meteor hooked up to this time...
It's all right...

...we'll be ready to go in a second. Just let me get rid of this nut-job in the spider costume first...
Ha ha ha! That would be a better name for him! I'll have to tell him when--

In and contain!
Move, move, move!
Oh no!
Wha--?

It happens in an instant--
--a blink of the eye--
--a tick of the clock--
NO!
VAAAAKT!

KRISSSHH!

Hey, I think I can see my house from--

Verily, thou dost venture much higher than usual this day, Spider-Man.
I get blasted through a skylight by a magnetized meteor and Thor just happens to be passing by?!
I'd heard that New York is lousy with super heroes these days, but what are the chances of catchin' one like a bus?
Um... uh...
Thor? Thor?!?
Uh... Yeah. Verily, Thor.

What misfortune set thee sky-ward, my friend?
The God of Thunder would aid you in your travails--and your foes would quake at the very sound of my voice!
Uh... yeah...that'd be good.
I don't know what's happened in the minute or two I've been gone--
--but maybe everybody will listen better to a bona fide Son of Asgard--
--Thor! The sky!?
Whatever Looter did to that meteor must've caused this!
Nay, friend! 'Tis not merely the work of human devices.

Thor hast seen the like of this before--
--and it chills his blood to see it again!

WUMWUMMMMM!
Stand by me, Spider-Man--that I may wield mystic Mjolnir and safeguard us from the coming cataclysm!

What is it, Thor? What're you doing?
WUMWUMMMMM!
I have transported us a half-step beyond the reality we know. For if yon anomaly is truly what I take it to be...

...t'would be better were we not within its chilling grasp.

Okay. Nothing's moving!
Time has stopped?!
Aye. 'Tis as I have viewed it before...
...aeons past, in the Realm of Asgard.

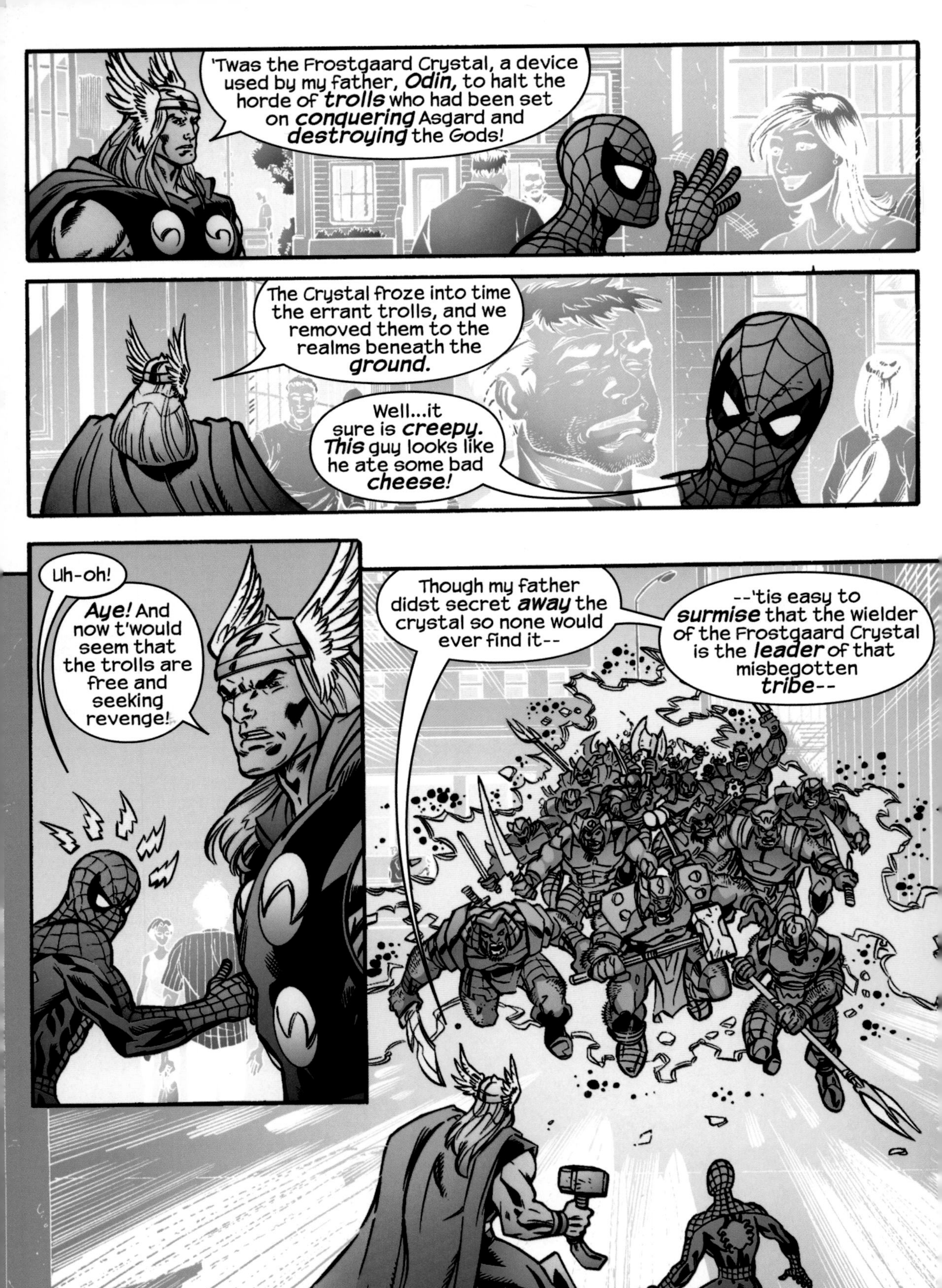
'Twas the Frostgaard Crystal, a device used by my father, Odin, to halt the horde of trolls who had been set on conquering Asgard and destroying the Gods!
The Crystal froze into time the errant trolls, and we removed them to the realms beneath the ground.
Well...it sure is creepy. This guy looks like he ate some bad cheese!
Uh-oh!
Aye! And now t'would seem that the trolls are free and seeking revenge!
Though my father didst secret away the crystal so none would ever find it--
--'tis easy to surmise that the wielder of the Frostgaard Crystal is the leader of that misbegotten tribe--

--the inaccurately dubbed Krylik the Conqueror!
You do me wrong, Odin-son! For without your godling brethren, without the warriors of your realm to stand beside you--

--I will bring you to your knees--
--and with you, all of Midgard shall fall. Then--on to Asgard!

Have at thee, Troll! For Thor is champion of Asgard and Midgard both--
--and I shall fight to my final breath--
--before I'd see either fall to the likes of you!!
WAM
Now I admit that sometimes I haven't got a clue what Thor is saying--

--and this Kryllk guy isn't too much better--
--but I'm pretty sure that "Midgard" means "Earth". And if that's what Thor is fighting for--

--then that's good enough for me!

Thou had best send in your good warriors, Kryllk--
WHUD!
CLUD!
--Thor is near done with these practice trolls!

Wow. Was that your idea of some Asgardian trash talk, Thor?
Oof!
Ungh!

Oot!
'Cause that was pathetic. You need to get with the times!
Kuhhh!

How art this...
"Dost thou desirest a piece of me?!"
That really loses something in the translation.
THWIP!
You gotta start watchin' more TV!
KLUNG!

Ah, I've enjoyed TV!
Mine favorite relates the antics of the short yellow man who lives under the sea...
...Robert-- the sponge with the straight trousers!
KRAK!
Ungh!

Oh, right. That's a good one.

You think it humorous, Odinson, to prattle on with your mortal lapdog while besting my warriors?
Hey!
It will be me laughing when I am seated on the Throne of Asgard--
--and your father serves as my lapdog!
Your dreams art fanciful, Troll Lord.
But Thor will make certain that thou shan't set one muddied boot in Asgard!
Ha ha ha-- you don't understand, pathetic godspawn-- with the Frostgaard Crystal at my command--
--I'm already there!
SWISSS
What is--
They vanish--like smoke!
Yeah, I've got the same problem over here. They're all disappearing.
SWISSSS
I must away!
'Tis my sworn duty to defend blessed Asgard at all costs.
I fear it may already be too late!
Hey! Count me in for a piece of that...
...you wouldn't wanna go anywhere without your favorite lapdog, wouldja?

Welcome then, friend-- to Asgard.
Would that it were on a happier occasion. Alas, it appears we hath arrived too late.
Wow! This is...is that...?

This is my father, Odin, the All-Father--
--and these, The Warriors Three!

Y'know, Thor-- I've got a question. We think we were too late--everything here is frozen...just like we left things back on Earth...
But if Kryllk got here ahead of us--
--then where is he?!

AAAHHHRRR!
T'would appear there is your answer!

Yeah, but that does raise some other questions, doesn't it?

Kryllk might have control of that dark crystal thing and he might be able to stop time and even be in two places at once...

...but so can we!
And with your little hammer ride , we can beat him to where he's going!
CLUD!

When you tried to hit him back on, uh, Midgard, he was gone--he was here...
...and I'll bet that if you try to pop him one here, he'll be there...

Do you mind? I'm trying to talk here.
But if you send me back, and we both take a poke at him at the same time...
Ungh!
KRAK!

Yea! I see the logic in your reasoning, friend!

Here then is thine transport, web-slinger.
May your boundless courage bring you boundless luck!

Right back atcha, Blondie!
And remember-- hit him at the same time!

Wait, Spider-Man--
--how shall we know?

Y'know, that's a very good question...
...I hadn't thought of that...

Soon...
Well, in a land where time is frozen it's pretty easy to find the only guys making any noise...
Now my problem is getting through to Kryllk to land a punch on him! His men are gonna make it hard!

And I'd better make it quick-- I can only assume that Thor's up in Asgard, wailin' away on his Kryllk, waiting for me to hit mine...
THWIP!

Asgard...
'Twas easier to beat a path to Kryllk before, when Spider-Man was at my side--
--now yon minions art focused only upon me!

I must make haste! Mayhap Spider-Man is e'en now battering at his incarnation of Kryllk--
--awaiting my blow!

'Scuse me! Pardon me! Comin' through!
WHAM!
BANG!
Betcha you guys never saw anything like *me* back in *Troll Land!*
SLAM!

And I'm gonna bet that you've never seen a *wrecking ball* either!
Heads *up,* trolls--

--it's time for a little *education!*
Ahhhhhhhhh!
SWWOOOOSH!

And now that I've taken your *ground troops* to school--
--it's time for some *aerial maneuvers!*

Enough! Begone, foul trolls! Though Asgard's time is stopped, mine doth run short!

'Tis your petulant leader that I take issue with--
KRA-KOWW!

--and I will be detained by this folly no longer!
SHKRAKKTAK!

To avoid having to contend with any more of his earthbound lot--
--mayhap mine next attack shouldst be from on high!

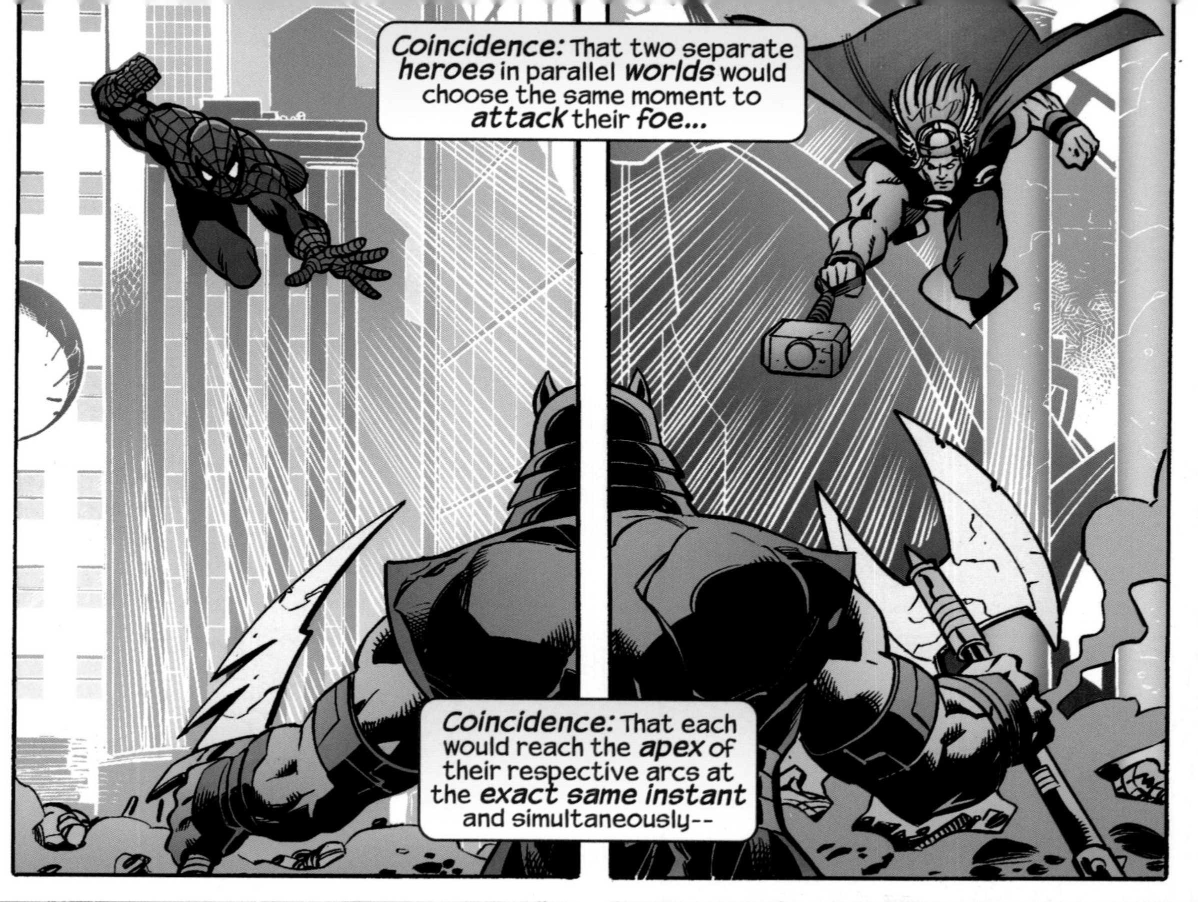
Coincidence: That two separate heroes in parallel worlds would choose the same moment to attack their foe...
Coincidence: That each would reach the apex of their respective arcs at the exact same instant and simultaneously--

--STRIKE!
WHAKK!
THWAKK!
UNHH!
UNHH!

Coincidence...? Perhaps...

But, then again, perhaps not.

Well, score one for the good guys!

We must have struck Kryllk at the same instant.

Looks like everything's going back to the way it was--
Hey, waitaminnit! I'm not s'posed to go! Why am I--

--fading?! As did Kryllk and his army?!
Why... Where--

What--?
Father. This was your summoning?

Aye, my son--being all-seeing, t'was soon that I realized what had transpired when you had vanquished foul Krylk!

Dost thou call us before you because you have another foe for us to smite?
Nay, Thor--not this time!
No, I called you here to sing thine praises!

Thou hast shown great courage and even greater intelligence in seeing through Krylk's devious scheme!
That he would escape his prison and acquire yon crystal were happenstances caused by the actions of a looting mortal's rock...

The Looter's meteor must've altered a magnetic field or something under Asgard...
Wow...who would've thought the Looter had it in 'im?
I applaud the actions of Thor and his... er...
...oddly garbed ally.

It is mine honor to serve you well, father. Your commendation is my reward!
Er... umm, yeah... thanks!
...uh, verily.
I return thee now, back to your world, back to the moment before the Crystal was activated and time was frozen.
Back?
No! Waitaminnit! All-Father-- Odin--
You have my thanks...and the gratitude of all of Asgard...
--NO!
Oh great.
Aw, not again!
Well, at least I'm pretty sure my old pal Thor is around here someplace...
sigh...
VAAAAKKT!
Next: X-Men's Storm!